Every day there's something new in Elmo's world!

Library of Congress Cataloging-in-Publication Data
Alexander, Liza. Giddy-up! / by Liza Alexander ; illustrated by David Prebenna.
p. cm. — (Elmo's world ; #1)
"Featuring Jim Henson's Sesame Street Muppets."
Summary: While waiting in line for his turn to ride a pony,
Elmo deals with his fears one by one.
ISBN 0-679-88697-4 (trade) — ISBN 0-679-98697-9 (lib. bdg.)
[1. Horses—Fiction. 2. Fear—Fiction. 3. Puppets—Fiction.]
I. Prebenna, David, ill. II. Title. III. Series.
PZ7.A37735Gi 1998
98-13301

www.randomhouse.com/kids
www.sesamestreet.com

Printed in the United States of America 10 9 8 7 6 5 4 3 2 1

Giddy-Up!

by Liza Alexander

illustrated by David Prebenna

Featuring Jim Henson's Sesame Street Muppets

CTW Books

Today is the day for pony rides.

Elmo and his mommy have been reading a book about ponies. Now Elmo is going to get to ride a real live pony—at last!

Elmo and all his friends are at the park. They wait in line for rides. Elmo sees the pony. She is furry. She is frisky. She is big! Elmo is glad there are so many people ahead of him in line.

Zoe is first. Upsy-do! "It's very high up there in the saddle," thinks Elmo.

Clip-clop, clip-clop. Zoe rides away.

The pony brings Zoe back. *Clip-clop, clip-clop,* STOP.
The pony nickers and flares her nostrils. "How will Zoe
ever get down?" wonders Elmo.

"Phew!" says Elmo. "There's a special steppy stool."

The pony man checks the pony's halter. The pony tosses her head back. "NEIGH!" she whinnies, and bares her gums.

"Those are very many teeth!" thinks Elmo.

Then Elmo remembers the cowboy book his mommy
read to him.

"Cowboys like to give their ponies big, shiny apples as treats," thinks Elmo.

Upsy-do! Up goes another rider onto the pony. Elmo is closer to the front of the line. The pony looks even bigger now. The pony stomps one heavy hoof. KLONK!

Elmo covers his ears. "Elmo does not like the noise of pony feet. Too loud! Maybe Elmo should go home now."

Elmo uncovers his ears. He looks at the pony's hooves again. Then he remembers, "Cowboys can teach ponies to count with their feet!"

The pony is back. Elmo looks at the pony's tail. It swings back and forth. SWISH! "What if the pony swats Elmo with her fat tail?"

"Nah! That won't happen. Ponies cooperate! Cowboys can even braid their ponies' tails!"

The pony man checks the saddle. The pony snuffles and puffs out her belly. She kicks. Elmo's eyes grow wide. He wonders, "Maybe that pony will toss Elmo—BOOM—on the ground. What if the pony is really a bucking bronco?"

"You know what?" Elmo asks himself. "That's all right, because cowboys know how to ride bucking broncos!"

Now it is Elmo's turn to ride the pony. "Here we go!" says his mommy. Elmo looks up at the pony and takes a deep breath.

"Okey-dokey," says Elmo. "Elmo is ready."

Upsy-do! Up goes Elmo into the saddle. He pats the pony's neck. It feels strong and soft and smooth. The saddle rocks gently as the pony walks calmly down the path. The pony does not bite or kick or buck. "You're a sweet little pony," says Elmo.

"Giddy-up!"

Every day there's something new in Elmo's world.
Today Elmo rode a pony for the first time.